Elliott's Talk

And Other Quicksolve Mini-Mysteries

Jim Sukach

Illustrated by Alan Flinn

Sterling Publishing Co., Inc.
New York

Quicksolve Mysteries™ is a trademark of James Richard Sukach

Library of Congress Cataloging-in-Publication Data

Sukach, Jim.
  Elliott's talking dog and other quicksolve mysteries / Jim Sukach ;
illustrated by Alan Flinn.
    p. cm.
  Includes index.
  ISBN 1-4027-2366-0
  1. Puzzles. 2. Detective and mystery stories. 3. Literary recreations. I.
Title.

GV1507.D4S8255 2005
793.73--dc22

2005019149

10 9 8 7 6 5 4 3 2 1

Published by Sterling Publishing Co., Inc.
387 Park Avenue South, New York, NY 10016
© 2005 by James Richard Sukach
Distributed in Canada by Sterling Publishing
c/o Canadian Manda Group, 165 Dufferin Street
Toronto, Ontario, Canada M6K 3H6
Distributed in Great Britain and Europe by Chris Lloyd at Orca Book
Services, Stanley House, Fleets Lane, Poole BH15 3AJ, England
Distributed in Australia by Capricorn Link (Australia) Pty. Ltd.
P.O. Box 704, Windsor, NSW 2756, Australia

Sterling ISBN 1-4027-2366-0

For information about custom editions, special sales, premium and
corporate purchases, please contact Sterling Special Sales
Department at 800-805-5489 or specialsales@sterlingpub.com.

Elliott's Talking Dog

CONTENTS

Dr. Jeffrey Lynn Quicksolve

Dr. Jeffrey Lynn Quicksolve is a university professor of criminology who retired from the police force at a young age after becoming famous as a brilliant detective. He still works with police agencies, private detectives, and his many friends solving crimes.

Dr. Quicksolve says, "The more you know about people and the world we live in, the easier it is to solve a problem."

Dr. Quicksolve's son, Junior, enjoys learning too, and he solves a few mysteries himself, often with the help of—or in spite of—his mischievous twin cousins, Flora and Fauna.

Detective Elliott Savant, who looks more like a mad scientist than a police detective with his long, curly black hair and his bushy black mustache, is a man of unusual intelligence and unique ability. His penchant for deep thinking sometimes leads him to forget certain things others might consider important, such as where he is and what he is doing at the moment. And so the quixotic detective has been assigned an assistant, the rather nervous Alvin Boysenberry, to look after him.

Elliott might arrive at a crime scene by motorcycle, wearing an unusual helmet with colorful plumes, or on Mollie, his dancing mule, with Marguerite, his cantankerous bulldog, trotting close behind. Elliott may playfully drive Officer Boysenberry to his wit's end, but he will solve the case, often in an unusual or hilarious manner. Join Dr. Quicksolve, Junior, and Detective Elliott Savant in their adventures, and solve these crimes along with them.

A Preference for Pontiacs

Dr. J. L. Quicksolve and Sergeant Rebekah Shurshot sat in a coffee shop on South University sipping tea and sharing a toasted sesame bagel. Sergeant Shurshot was explaining that what looked like a series of robberies might not be.

"Looks like? Might not be?" Dr. Quicksolve said.

"Yes, well," Sergeant Shurshot said. "There was a holdup in Pittsfield at a gas station on Michigan Avenue a week ago. The robber used a gun and wore a ski mask. The clerk could only say it was a tall, thin man, six feet two or three. That was all he could say. He did see the car, though, even though it was dark. It was a red Pontiac Grand Am. He even got the license number."

"That's a lot of information to get in the dark. How did he manage it?" Dr. Quicksolve asked.

"Well, he said the robber had backed his car up to the door for a fast getaway. It was easy to see the car and the license plate before he got away. That doesn't seem too smart on the crook's part, does it?" Sergeant Shurshot asked.

"It almost sounds as if he wanted the clerk to get his license number," Dr. Quicksolve said.

"Well," Sergeant Shurshot continued, "we checked the number, and it belongs to a seventy-five-year-old man who lives on the west side of town, about eight miles away. He has an alibi. He was home playing Ping-Pong with his wife. His daughter and her husband were there, too. The car was parked in front of the house. It was seen by a neighbor at the time of the robbery."

"That's interesting," Dr. Quicksolve said. He took a sip of his tea and stared out the window at the people walking by. It was a cold day, and people held onto their hats and clutched their coats close to themselves against the chilly, fall wind.

"There's more," Sergeant Shurshot said. "Last week a similar robbery occurred on the west side of town. It also involved a tall robber with a ski mask and gun. He also backed up to the door of a convenience store, this time in a Pontiac Firebird. The clerk wrote down the license plate number as the robber got into his car and drove off. It seems like too much of a coincidence to not be the same guy, yet he did use two different cars. We traced the license to a teenager who was at a football game in Lansing. He said he left his car in the high school parking lot in town. It was there when he left, and it was there when he got back."

"Also at night?" Dr. Quicksolve asked.

"Yes. The whole thing happened a third time, on the north side of town."

"The getaway car?"

"A blue Pontiac Bonneville."

"Let me guess," said Dr. Quicksolve. "It belonged to someone else who had a good alibi."

"That is right," Sergeant Shurshot said. "Do you think this guy is stealing their cars and bringing them back? It seems like the cars are in two places at once."

"Let's stake out the Pontiac dealerships in the area," Dr. Quicksolve said.

What did Dr. Quicksolve think was going on?

Answer on page 75.

Suspicious Circumstances

Junior Quicksolve grabbed his backpack full of school books and an apple from the refrigerator. He called out, "Come on, Dad!" and ran out to the garage where he got into his father's yellow VW Beetle. Dr. J. L. Quicksolve poured coffee into his travel thermos and secured the top before following Junior to the garage.

On the drive to school Junior said, "Look at that sports car!" The sunlight gleamed brightly off the shiny red car parked on the side of Ellsworth Road. Dr. Quicksolve looked at the car and noticed a man in a light raincoat standing near it on the edge of the road. He turned toward the bushes as they drove by. Dr. Quicksolve saw another man sitting in a car parked in front of the sports car. The detective pulled to the side of the road. He reached for his cell phone, called the police, and reported a possible car theft in progress and gave their location.

Almost immediately, a siren was heard. The man by the car threw something into the bushes and ran to the car with the man sitting in it. Dr. Quicksolve jumped out of his car and signaled the policeman. The policeman pulled up in front of them before they could pull away and apprehended them. The two men were arrested and placed in the police car.

Dr. Quicksolve talked briefly to the police officer and then he got back into his car. He and Junior pulled away, heading for school again. Junior turned to his father and asked, "How did you know they were going to steal that car?"

How did Dr. Quicksolve know?

Answer on page 73.

Rainy Day Deli

Packing up in a rain shower after a week at Boy Scout camp was not a lot of fun. Fortunately, this was the last day of camp for Dr. J. L. Quicksolve and his son Junior, who were helping some Cub Scouts. The week had been a good one with lots of sun and fun. The rain had begun in the middle of the last night.

Now, though, Dr. Quicksolve and Junior were the last two people to leave, taking down the last tent. They made an eerie sight—two dark, shapeless forms in their rain parkas. It was a gray day. Everything looked gray, blurred by the sheets of rain pouring down relentlessly as the two figures quietly moved around, pulling tent stakes and taking the tent down into a puddle of water. It would have to be spread out in the garage at home and taken out to dry in the sunlight—whenever there was sunlight again.

They finally got everything packed in or tied to the top of Dr. Quicksolve's VW Beetle. They climbed in, glad to get out of the rain, and they headed toward one of Junior's favorite places, a small grocery and deli on North Territorial Road, a long, winding two-lane road that led to the freeway. Junior could hardly wait to get one of their huge deli sandwiches.

As they pulled into the parking lot, they saw two police cars and the car of a park ranger already there.

When they went in, they found out that the store had been robbed. A county deputy recognized Dr. Quicksolve and told him what had happened.

"There was a stickup," the deputy explained. "Two guys came in and ordered sandwiches. When the owner went to make the sandwiches, the robbers grabbed the money out of the cash register and drove off. The owner didn't get a good look at the men, but he described the car, and we nabbed a couple of suspects down the freeway about three miles."

"These isolated places close to the freeway can be sitting ducks," another deputy said.

The first deputy continued. "Our man out there has talked to the suspects. They claim they were at Camp Pioneer, about three miles from here, for the night. They said they drove by here, but didn't stop."

"Camp Pioneer is a place for serious campers. It has dirt roads and no facilities, except for one old outhouse," the park ranger said.

Did they have camping gear?" Junior asked.

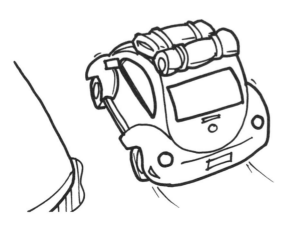

"Good question," the park ranger said.

"No, as a matter of fact," the first deputy said. "But they claim they just stopped there to rest. They said they slept in the car. They said they knew few people went there and it would be a quiet place to rest."

"Well, we need to see the car," Dr. Quicksolve said. "That will tell us something about whether they're telling us the truth or not."

What would the car tell them?

Answer on page 76.

Beekerjar's First Case

Some readers have questioned the spelling of Science Officer Beekerjar's name, as if I just make these names up. Their question has to do with the fact that a science beaker is spelled b-e-a-k-e-r. That is right, but the fact that Officer Beekerjar's name sounds like "beaker jar" is merely a coincidence. Of course, the fact that his name sounds like something out of a science lab might well have influenced Beanie's choice of a career. Others question my use of the phrase "Science Officer." This is what Science Officer Beekerjar calls himself. Who am I to argue? He said he was a longtime fan of the original Star Trek series, and he particularly admired Mr. Spock, the Science Officer. Beanie Beekerjar is actually related to the famous Beekerjars of Caro, Michigan, Bean Capital of the World. Beanie's father, of course, was the Bean King himself. That is why Officer Beekerjar was named Beanie, and that is why he wants to be called Officer Beekerjar.

Little Beanie's father was disappointed that his son didn't want to follow in his footsteps and become Bean Prince of the World. But Beanie Beekerjar had other plans and hoped to get out from under his father's thumb. Some people will understand what I mean by that better than others. It really all began with the incident with Mrs. Winthrop's cow.

Mrs. Winthrop lived alone just off Highway 24 near Cat Lake. Her husband, the late Mr. Winthrop, had been an accountant. Their friends liked to call him "the bean counter," a local joke. He had left Mrs. Winthrop a nice portfolio of stocks and a fair amount of money in the bank. Mrs. Winthrop liked to save her money for the proverbial "rainy day" and hated to take anything out of her bank account. So when Rachel, her cow, stopped giving milk every morning, she was quite upset. "Rachel is in good health and should be giving milk just fine," the veterinarian said. "In fact, it looks like she is being milked regularly."

Mrs. Winthrop was very suspicious and decided to hire Beanie and his friend Cole to stay in the barn and watch Rachel for her. She hoped to catch whoever was stealing milk.

Beanie and Cole came out to look things over. Beanie already had quite a collection of things he carried around in a brown suitcase to use in his crime detection. Mrs. Winthrop

showed the boys where Rachel spent her time in a small pasture. Beanie noticed a set of large footprints that went out to Rachel's favorite standing place. There was a set of what looked like dog prints in the soft ground alongside the shoeprints that went directly out to Rachel's spot.

When Mrs. Winthrop said they were not there yesterday, Beanie had an idea. He spoke up confidently. "I can check three things here that will help us catch the thief."

What three things?

Answer on page 75.

Just a Touch

Dr. J. L. Quicksolve did not like getting to a crime scene so late after it had been discovered, but he had been riding his motorcycle in the Irish Hills with Junior when he got the message on his cell phone that Jack Combs, a wealthy beekeeper from Stony Creek, had apparently committed suicide at his farm five miles south of Ann Arbor.

When Dr. Quicksolve and his son arrived on the scene, the body was gone. Officer Longarm was in the kitchen talking to Jack's wife, Honey.

As they stood in front of the computer desk, Officer

Lurkin and Sergeant Shurshot talked to Dr. Quicksolve. Officer Lurkin said, "His body was found hunched over his computer keyboard. There was a typed note on the desk beside him. It said he discovered that his wife was planning to leave him and that she was in love with Sam Stones, his business partner."

"What did Officer Beekerjar find out?" Dr. Quicksolve asked.

"He said Combs died from some kind of poison. He hasn't figured out what kind of poison yet," Officer Lurkin said. "He also found three fingerprints from the deceased on the front of the note."

"No other fingerprints?" Dr. Quicksolve said.

"Just three across the top on the front of the page," Officer Lurkin repeated.

"Who found the body?" Dr. Quicksolve asked.

"His wife said she was out shopping. She came home and found her husband dead at his computer. She said she was distraught when she found him and read the note. She called the hospital for an ambulance. Then she called the police. She said she was afraid to touch anything," Officer Lurkin explained.

"Did she admit to being in love with Stone?" Dr. Quicksolve said.

"She said they bowled together," Officer Lurkin said.

"It does look bad for Mrs. Combs and Sam Stone, even though they tried to throw us off track," Dr. Quicksolve said.

What did Dr. Quicksolve mean?

Answer on page 76.

B & P Laundry

"**H**e was found near the shore of the lake about two hundred yards from his cottage, after someone tried to drown him," Sergeant Rebekah Shurshot told Dr. J. L. Quicksolve as they drove through town. "It's a miracle he's still alive. He's in the hospital and is expected to recover. We suspect his partner, Reggie Pigeoncoff. We learned they were having quite a dispute about how to run their laundry business. Pigeoncoff thought Bartlette was stealing from the company and buying stocks and bonds for himself."

"So, we're driving to the cottage now?" Dr. Quicksolve asked.

"Yes," Sergeant Shurshot said, "but I thought we should stop at Bartlette's bank first."

"Why his bank?" Dr. Quicksolve asked.

"On the way to pick you up, I got a call from Officer Longarm. He's at the bank now. The bank manager told him Pigeoncoff was in the safe deposit box area yesterday. Bartlette has a box there too. The manager said Pigeoncoff was only in the room with the boxes for a short time. He came out looking very angry, threw a piece of paper on the floor, and marched out. We also found out that he purchased an airline ticket to Buenos Aires, departing Metro Airport at six o'clock today. We're hoping to find a reason to stop him."

"Well, what was on the paper he threw down at the bank?" Dr. Quicksolve said.

"Numbers," Sergeant Shurshot said. She looked at her notepad. "1-20-12-1-11-5-19-20-15-16-16. The bank manager said the boxes have numbers and combination locks, but not as many numbers as this. They can't be a box number and combination."

"Let me see the numbers," Dr. Quicksolve said.

Sergeant Shurshot handed her notebook to Dr. Quicksolve. He looked at it and said, "Have someone arrest Pigeoncoff, and let's go to the hospital and see how Bartlette is doing."

What had Dr. Quicksolve figured out?

Answer on page 74.

Bomb Threats

The bomb threats came from the pay phone in a small diner two miles outside town. All six targets were government buildings in the city. The police responded quickly, and no bombs were found. The calls were traced to the diner, and the police surrounded the isolated building.

By the time Dr. J. L. Quicksolve arrived in his yellow VW Beetle, the officers had everything under control, though they hadn't yet identified the caller from the people in the diner.

Officer Lurkin met Dr. Quicksolve in front of the restaurant. "We have five people in here," Officer Lurkin began, "but no one's talking. At least, no one can say for sure who used the telephone by the door where the calls were made. Officer Beekerjar is checking for fingerprints right now."

They entered the front door and saw Officer Beekerjar standing by the telephone that hung on the wall. A yellow telephone book hung from a chain next to the phone. "This is the phone that was used. We traced the call. It looks like the caller wiped the phone clean of fingerprints. I'm still checking for things."

Dr. Quicksolve and Officer Lurkin walked into the restaurant. Five people sat at five separate tables. A police officer sat next to each one. No one was talking. Sergeant Shurshot walked over to Dr. Quicksolve and Officer Lurkin and said, "We can't tell who was on the phone. The waitress left for a cigarette. The busboy walked out to use his cell phone. One customer went to buy a newspaper. We can't get the times

straight for sure. Someone could have stepped in to use the phone. We don't have much to go on right now."

"I don't suppose there would be fingerprints on the coins in the machine," Officer Lurkin suggested.

"Fingerprints are a good idea," Dr. Quicksolve replied. "There is one place to check before we look at coins, though."

Where was Dr. Quicksolve suggesting they look for the fingerprints of the caller?

Answer on page 77.

Mr. Seeotu's Briefcase

Junior Quicksolve got to his middle school early to practice shooting hoops in the gym. As he approached the front door, he was surprised to see Sergeant Rebekah Shurshot's black and white police car. The front doors of the school had been unlocked, but Junior didn't see anyone else in the building until he turned down the hall to his locker, which was next to his science room—Mr. Seeotu's room. There he saw Sergeant Shurshot, in uniform, talking to Miss Laptop, the principal's secretary, and to Mr. Seeotu. Junior began to listen. Following in his famous father's footsteps, Junior had established a reputation for himself by single-handedly solving several mysteries around town, and he was welcome to join the adults.

"I called Travis, the night custodian," Miss Laptop said. "He said he began cleaning this corridor after everyone had left the building. He said Mr. Seeotu's briefcase was on his desk when he cleaned and when he left the room. He finished this room., took his break, then came back and finished the rest of the rooms here. He said he locked the building even before he cleaned this room. He didn't see anyone else in the building all evening."

"What was in your briefcase, Mr. Seeotu?" Sergeant Shurshot asked.

"I just had a couple of biology books and the test for today's semester exam," Mr. Seeotu said. He seemed quite nervous about what was happening. "I don't know if this is really police business," he said.

"Well," Miss Laptop said, "your briefcase is missing—

probably stolen. If something's stolen, it's right to call the police."

Junior walked into the classroom while they continued to talk. It looked the same as it always did in the morning. The desks stood in neat rows. The floor shone and the chalkboard had been washed clean. Junior stepped into Mr. Seeotu's small office. It was as usual too—quite a mess. There were test tubes and papers on the counter by the window. Piles of papers and books were all over the desk. Pencil shavings lay on the floor beneath the sharpener attached to the wall just inside the door. Everything was normal. Junior walked out of the office and back to the classroom door.

"I saw John Bigdood in front of the building late yesterday," Junior said. "I was studying in the city library across the street. Is John in your class, Mr. Seeotu?"

"Yes. He's on my class list, but he's absent more than he's here," Mr. Seeotu said. "He'd be a good suspect. He has to pass this test if he's going to pass the class, and he knows it."

"You saw him in front of the building?" Sergeant Shurshot asked Junior.

"Yes. I didn't really see him leaving the building," Junior said.

"How could he have been in the building if Travis locked up after everyone left?" Miss Laptop asked. "Where could he have been? Travis eats lunch at my desk so he can use the office phone to talk to his girlfriend." No one knew how Miss Laptop had this piece of information. No one questioned her. "He can see the main hall and the front doors and the entrance to this hall. No one could have come into this hall without being seen by Travis."

"Unless . . . ," Junior said.

Unless what?

Answer on page 75.

29

Stolen Medals

Dr. J. L. Quicksolve hadn't heard from his friend Fred Fraudstop in quite some time. Fred Fraudstop worked for an insurance company that insured valuables. He investigated claims that often involved crimes, and when he was in trouble he called Dr. Quicksolve. Dr. Quicksolve met his friend at the home of Olympic champion swimmer Susie Splash.

Standing in the library of Susie's beautiful home, Dr. Quicksolve liked what he saw. The room had a high ceiling, a cozy fireplace, and walls all lined with books. A hardwood floor was covered with Persian rugs, and two large, comfortable leather chairs faced the fireplace. It was a room for quiet reading, study, and intimate conversation. It seemed so familiar and cozy to Dr. Quicksolve, he half expected to see his own copy of *The Poetry of Robert Frost* lying beside it.

The broken window was a glaring contradiction to the ambience of the room—an unforgivable intrusion. Even more unforgivable was that Susie's three gold medals had been stolen from the fireplace mantel.

Dr. Quicksolve looked at the broken window, the only window in the room. It was on the wall directly across from the fireplace, behind the high-back chairs. There was a small hole broken just above the latch. It could have been done fairly quietly.

"I was sitting in front of the fireplace reading," Susie told the two men. "The phone rang. My husband and I have only two telephones, one upstairs in our bedroom and the other one in the kitchen at the opposite end of the house. We have it that way on purpose, so we won't be disturbed when we want a quiet time to read or talk. I could barely hear it ring because I was playing music. I wasn't going to answer it—there's an answering machine, but I decided it might be my husband, who's out of town. No one was on the line."

"I noticed one car in the driveway," Dr. Quicksolve said. "Is that yours?"

"Yes. My husband took his car on his business trip," Susie said. "This all happened when I was out of the room answering the phone. I didn't hear anything, but when I returned, the window was broken, and I noticed immediately that the medals were gone. I don't know who could have stolen them like that—so quickly."

"Olympic medals, especially a set of three gold medals, would be very valuable to certain unscrupulous collectors," Fred Fraudstop said. "I think it would be a professional who did this."

"Or someone connected to a professional, and someone connected to you," Dr. Quicksolve said to Susie. "We need a list of everyone who has been in the house recently, and I'd like to see your telephone."

Why the list? Why the telephone?

Answer on page 74.

Elliott's Talking Dog

Officer Alvin Boysenberry drove his black and white police car slowly along the street on the edge of the park, looking for Detective Elliott Savant. He saw a crowd ahead, obviously following a tall, thin man with bushy black hair who was walking a brown and white bulldog on a leash. He was apparently having quite a conversation with the dog, and a crowd of kids walking along and following on bicycles was fascinated by the situation, laughing and enjoying themselves.

As he got closer, Officer Boysenberry could see Elliott looking down at his bulldog, Marguerite. Marguerite would then look up at Elliott, smile, and actually appear to move her lips as a high-pitched voice seemed to come from her in response to Elliott's comment. The kids roared with laughter. Boysenberry smiled; he too had been fooled the first time he saw Elliott throw his voice so it looked like Marguerite was carrying on a conversation with him. Elliott was a ventriloquist, and he had trained Marguerite to flex her lips into a smile, as if she were talking to him. Boysenberry stopped his car and gently tapped his horn to get Elliott's attention. The kids were disappointed when Elliott and Marguerite trotted over and hopped into the police car.

"We're supposed to follow a new guy in town who we think is buying stolen items from local hoodlums. His name is Slim Bones. He's from Chicago, and he's meeting a couple of guys from Detroit at a bar on the south side of town. The Detroit guys are named Starch and Coils. Officer Lurkin is there now. We need to meet him."

The three of them walked into the dark and smoky bar and headed for Officer Lurkin. He told them he was watching three men sitting at a table across the room. He said he didn't know which one was Slim, but he thought the bartender knew the men. "So let's talk to the bartender," a squeaky voice from the floor piped up. Officer Lurkin jumped with surprise and looked down at Marguerite, who smiled back at him. "Don't look so surprised, Big Guy," Marguerite seemed to say. "I'm workin' undercover."

Boysenberry chuckled quietly, and Elliott kept a straight face as he looked around the room nonchalantly. "Call the bartender over here," Marguerite said.

Officer Lurkin looked at Marguerite and Boysenberry and then at Elliott, but he didn't say anything to them. He signaled the bartender with his hand, and the bartender walked to their end of the bar. "Yeah?" he said.

"Those three guys look familiar to me," Officer Lurkin said. "Isn't that Slim Bones?" He nodded his head to indicate the man on their right, a slim man in a black leather jacket. "And that's Starch in the middle and Coils on the other side?"

"You got the names right, but you put them with all the wrong guys," the bartender said. Just then someone at the other end of the bar called for the bartender, and he walked away. Then the man in the middle stood up and turned left to the first man and said, "Let's go, Starch." They walked out of the bar and walked to the left. The third man followed them and turned to the right.

Elliott stood up, and he and Marguerite walked toward the door. Elliott stopped. Marguerite turned back and said, "Let's go, guys," with that squeaky voice.

Which way did Elliott and Marguerite go?

Answer on page 77.

Litter and Larceny

Many groups "adopt" portions of highways. This means they accept responsibility for occasionally getting together to walk along a particular stretch of road and pick up litter and trash that has accumulated along the side.

Detective Elliott Savant and his young friends Junior Quicksolve and Prissy Powers did things differently. They randomly chose sections of country roads to clean up. What made the chore fun for them was that they got to enjoy the country outings and be in nature. They also enjoyed the company of the animals they brought along to help.

Elliott's famous dancing mule, Mollie, always led the way, with Elliott on her back, of course. Mollie was as large as a horse and quite handsome. The distinguishing features were her big ears, where Elliott had attached large, round, yellow reflectors so oncoming drivers could see them as they approached. Always safety conscious, Elliott wore a feather-plumed helmet, which he also wore when he rode his motorcycle. He was a sight, with his long coat and galoshes and the brightly colored feathers sticking straight up from his black helmet. Behind Elliott and Mollie, Junior and Prissy rode their own horses, two beautiful, golden Tennessee walking horses. The horses were Corky and Dusty. Behind them trotted Marguerite, Elliott's irascible bulldog, and Copper, Junior's rust-colored retriever.

When they decided on a stretch of road, they would stop and dismount. The two dogs would get right to work, scouting the brush along the road for litter. Marguerite would find paper bags and cups, etc. Then she would bark for Copper, who would frolic over, get the item, and take it to someone to put into a bag. Actual retrieving was beneath Marguerite's dignity.

This wonderful spring had begun with a beautiful sunrise, and it was peaceful and quiet out now in the country. They rambled along the country road for hours, stopping for a little picnic lunch and continuing on into late afternoon.

They had filled about five bags with litter, which they attached to their saddles, when they saw the dust of an approaching vehicle. It was a mail truck that stopped at each mailbox to deposit letters. The next car came up much faster. The car looked very familiar, a black and white police car,

which turned onto a long driveway ahead of them. They decided to see what was going on and looked down a long driveway that led to a large, secluded house. Three police cars were parked in front of the house.

Junior and Prissy took care of the animals, and Elliott walked up to the house. Officer Longarm was there. He told Elliott that Sergeant Rebekah Shurshot was inside, talking to the owners, Tom and Lisa Hogback, who had had two valuable paintings stolen from them early that morning.

"Were they home?" Elliott asked.

"Yes," Officer Longarm said. "Mrs. Hogback was still asleep. Mr. Hogback said he had been up for about an hour and had decided to walk out to the road to get the mail. He said the paintings were there when he left and gone when he got back. He said that behind his house was a driveway that was used by several property owners and that led to another road, one the thieves could have used as an escape route. He couldn't explain how the burglars knew just when he would be out, unless they were somehow watching him."

"The timing is a problem that makes this story unbelievable right at the moment," Elliott said.

What did Elliott find so unbelievable about the timing?

Answer on page 76.

A Stolen Car and a Long Walk

Detective Elliott Savant loved to ride his motorcycle on the segment of Huron River Drive that snaked along the river and ran north and west toward the "Chain of Lakes" connected by the river. He enjoyed the serene, tree-lined road and the warm summer sun.

Elliott's bulldog, Marguerite, may have been enjoying the ride even more. She stood with her hind legs on the seat of the sidecar. Her front paws stretched up to the front of the cockpit area behind a small windshield. Her helmeted head and goggled eyes peeked over the top of the windshield. Her lips were splayed by the wind of the racing motorcycle, causing what appeared to be a broad smile and happy relief from the summer heat.

Elliott's hands spread out on the handlebar grips. His helmet was topped with a large, brightly colored plume of orange and yellow and purple feathers that fluttered and danced in the wind.

Elliott felt a tingling vibration on his chest. He reached into his shirt pocket and retrieved his cell phone. He pulled his motorcycle off to the side of the road to talk on the phone. Marguerite sat back on her seat and waited patiently.

Officer Longarm told Elliott that a recently stolen car had been spotted at the Portage Lake Convenience Store, which was only eight miles away. The car had been stolen at a gas station earlier, when the owner left her keys inside when she went to pay for the gasoline.

Elliott slapped a round magnetic light to the top of Marguerite's helmet. He pressed a switch, and the red light began to flash. Elliott pressed another switch that caused a siren to wail, and they were on their way.

Elliott arrived at the convenience store, and Officer Longarm explained the situation. He said a county deputy had pulled into the store parking lot and noticed the car. He called in that he had found a stolen car. The store clerk said the most recent customers were three teenagers—a girl and two boys. They were wearing swimsuits, tee shirts, and sandals. They bought three cans of soda, and were walking

down the road when the deputy arrived. The deputy was patrolling the area, looking for them.

Officer Longarm's car radio began to squawk, and he walked over to his car to listen. The deputy had found three teenagers who matched the clerk's description. Elliott and Marguerite jumped into the police car, and they drove off.

They found the deputy's car about three miles away on the side of the road. He was talking to three teenagers in swimsuits and tee shirts. One of the boys still had a can of soda in his hand and a towel wrapped around his shoulders.

"How are we going to prove they stole the car?" Officer

Longarm asked as he stopped his car. "Should I radio for Officer Beekerjar to check for fingerprints?"

"Good idea," Elliott said, "but there may not be fingerprints. There might be something else, though. They might be foolish enough to have evidence on them right now."

Officer Longarm looked at the three teenagers in swimsuits. He shook his head and said, "Where?"

Where, indeed? Why not fingerprints?

Answer on page 78.

My Stolen Car Case

I don't usually put myself in a story, but since I was there with Detective Elliott Savant, I thought I might as well just tell the story the way it happened.

In addition to writing, I also work part-time jobs occasionally. I told Elliott about a job I had testing Hardman Sand Soap, and he said he'd like to help. Hardman Sand Soap is a special formula for people who have very dirty jobs and have a tough time getting clean after working with tar, paint, glue, and other substances. The company found the best way to test their new formulas was to have volunteers lie down in the waters of the Huron River. The river scum that baked onto the volunteers' skin proved quite a challenge for the soap manufacturer. The current formula took it off after a lot of scrubbing, but the abrasion did more harm than good.

So Elliott and I headed for the river on the shore of Riverside Park. I told Elliott the river was no more than three feet deep, but he insisted on wearing a snorkel and large yellow swim fins. We lay down in the cold, murky green water. I kept my head out of the water. Elliott disappeared below the surface. Only the snorkel could be seen sticking up out of the water beside me.

I saw a black and white police car approaching us. It stopped on the edge of the river, and Sergeant Rebekah Shurshot got out of the car and called us to come to the shore. When I stood up in the shallow water, it felt as if I were covered in plastic wrap. The water didn't roll off me in drops but seemed to stay on my body, clinging more tightly as it began to dry in the sun. I tried shaking myself like a dog, but that didn't work either. I still felt coated in oil. Elliott made his way to shore awkwardly, and I followed.

Sergeant Shurshot told us the woman in the back seat of the police car claimed her car had just been stolen by a man with a gun.

"Did you call in a description of the stolen car?" Elliott asked.

"Yes. It was a 1957 red Thunderbird with a white convertible top," Sergeant Shurshot said. "The woman said she was going to her car after shopping at the mall. The man came up

behind her and grabbed her by the arm. He showed her that he had a gun and demanded her purse and keys. She gave them to him, and he drove off. She ran into the mall and called the police.

"Did she have a lot of money?" Elliott asked.

"She didn't have much in her purse. She had credit cards, a cell phone, and a diamond ring she had taken off to try on other rings at a jewelry store in the mall. She said she tossed her ring into her purse and forgot to put it back on when she left the jewelry store.

"Interesting," Elliott said. He walked to the police car like a duck learning to walk.

I thought I might have a chance to actually solve this one, so I began asking Sergeant Shurshot a few questions. Before I really had much figured out, Elliott came walking back toward us, talking on his cell phone. It sounded like he was buying a used car.

"Yes," he said into the small device. "I'm interested in the car you have for sale. I read about it in the newspaper. If it's in good shape, I'll pay the full price you ask."

"What a great idea!" Sergeant Shurshot whispered excitedly into my ear.

What was the great idea?

46

Beach Bandits

Dogs were not allowed on the stretch of sandy beach along the edge of Silver Lake, but you could take your dog on the large grassy area a little up from the lake. Sunbathers crowded both areas. Detective Elliott Savant sat next to blonde-haired Rookie Officer B. Hope Peterson on a blanket in the grassy area. Marguerite, Elliott's bulldog, sat between them. Rookie Officer Peterson wore a black two-piece swimsuit. Elliott felt comfortable with the natural way Officer Peterson behaved on the beach as an undercover officer. She appeared to be someone just enjoying a day at the beach, yet he could tell she was very much aware what was happening around them.

Detective Elliott Savant, though, dressed in long shorts that served as his swimsuit, had a little more trouble fooling the public simply because he had become known to many people who recognized his black curly hair and bushy mustache, not to mention his dog, Marguerite.

"This is the area where most of the wallets have been stolen," Officer Peterson said. "Some days it happens nearly once every hour or so, and no one has seen it happen yet."

"There must be some . . ." Elliott began when there was a sudden uproar of barking dogs. They looked down the beach to see a man walking five or six dogs of various breeds and sizes. He strained to hold them back on their leashes as he walked through the crowd of sunbathers.

Suddenly, two burly young men in swimsuits, who had been lying quietly on a blanket on the sand, began arguing and shouting at each other. They began to wrestle in the sand, and the sunbathers ran to watch the fight. Two sunbathers grabbed one man by the arms and held him back. Elliott and Officer Peterson held the other. The two men gradually quieted down and indicated the fight was over.

Elliott, Officer Peterson, and Marguerite went back to their blanket. A woman who had been lying next to them began to look frantically through her things. "My wallet has been stolen!" she said.

No one had seen a thing. Officer Peterson was upset. "I can't believe this happened! Right here! Right next to us!"

"Let's be patient," Elliott said. He was standing on his head with his legs pointing straight up. "Let's get a hot dog," he said. Elliott stood up and started walking toward the concession stand. A frustrated Officer Peterson marched behind him. A very happy Marguerite, who had heard "hot dog," pranced behind her.

Elliott bought three hot dogs. He put mustard on two of them, and then he took his wallet out of his pocket and carefully spread mustard across the inside of it. He took several rubber bands out and put them tightly around his wallet. He called Marguerite, who had finished her hot dog quickly, and he held the wallet down for her to smell. He walked back to the blanket, munching his hot dog and then dropped his wallet into his shoe, which was on the blanket. He sat down just as they heard the now-familiar barking of the dogs being walked by the man with the leashes. They were coming back from the other direction.

What was Elliott doing?

Answer on page 75.

Dead Ringer

Mollie was a handsome mule. Really, she looked like a large brown horse with big ears. Some say mules are stubborn. People who are better informed know that mules are smart and consider what they do before they do it. Fortunately, Mollie liked to dance and welcomed the chance to show off in parades, as she was doing now. She walked sideways to the right and left, backed in a circle, and bowed to the crowd every block or two as the parade laced its way through town.

Detective Elliott Savant enjoyed the show too. He was wearing his sombrero and cowboy outfit, that included his famous sheepskin chaps that covered his legs like gobs of mashed potatoes. He rode through the parade on Mollie.

A uniformed police officer raced out of the crowd and up to Elliott. "There's been a robbery and a murder downtown!" Officer Alvin Boysenberry shouted frantically.

"Well, let's go," Elliott said, leaning forward and offering his hand to Boysenberry, who reached up and grabbed it without thinking. Mollie, who knew what was happening, braced herself and stepped forward as Elliott pulled, and Boysenberry went flying through the air and landed on Mollie right behind Elliott. They turned and galloped toward the center of town.

Three police cars and an ambulance were parked in front of the jewelry store. Officers were cordoning off the area with yellow police tape to keep the crowd of onlookers back.

Elliott didn't have to show identification. Everyone on the force knew who he was, even with his cowboy outfit and mule (or maybe because of his cowboy outfit and mule).

Elliott and Boysenberry were greeted by Officer Longarm. Behind him they could see Matthew and Mattie, two police medics. They were covering a body that lay in the middle of the floor.

"Is that the jewelry store owner?" Boysenberry asked.

"That's right," Officer Longarm said. He gave Elliott all the details they knew. "It looks like someone walked in and shot him."

"That's it?" Boysenberry said.

"No," Officer Longarm said. "Let me go on. We have a video. It doesn't show much. It shows the jeweler turning toward the opening door. We see an arm sticking out and pointing the gun at him. Then we only see the shoulder of the assailant as he walks along the wall and disappears from sight altogether. He emptied all the cabinets and showcases along the wall where a lot of the expensive items were kept."

"Can we see the recording?" Elliott asked.

"Yes. Let's go into the back," Officer Longarm said, and he led them to a small, dark room at the back of the store. "There's just the one camera," Officer Longarm said. He turned on a television, and they watched the murder take place just as the officer had described.

"Not much to go on," Boysenberry said.

"Only that it was probably an inside job," Elliott said, "an employee or someone who knows an employee."

Why did Elliott suspect an employee?

Answer on page 76.

Benjamin Clayborn Blowhard

Benjamin Clayborn Blowhard was a friend of Sergeant Rebekah Shurshot and for that reason he was tolerated by a few others. He dressed the part of the great world adventurer he saw himself to be. His cowboy hat was pinned up on one side and tied under his chin with what he said was a shark's tooth slide. He wore a khaki jungle jacket with loops for shotgun shells, and his alligator boots displayed him to the world as a man who had been there and back. The monocle he wore over one eye aided the exotic air he was looking for. He told stories to prove he was the man he appeared to be, but were his stories true?

Grandpa Blowhard's Mules

Junior Quicksolve and his twin cousins, Flora and Fauna, sat side by side on the corral fence. They were watching Detective Elliott Savant practice twirling his lasso over his head while standing up straight on Mollie, his famous dancing mule, as she walked around in a large circle. Elliott was dressed in his cowboy outfit, complete with wool chaps and bright red cowboy boots. Mollie, a well-trained mule, kept a steady pace, which she gradually increased at Elliott's command.

Benjamin Clayborn Blowhard drove his Humvee SUV up to the fence and stopped in a cloud of dust. He got out of the huge military-style vehicle quickly, before the dust settled, and began walking toward the threesome. He liked the dramatic effect of walking out of the dust cloud, because he saw himself as an action movie hero.

"We're going to hear a story now," Flora whispered.

"Quite a story," Fauna said.

Blowhard watched what Elliott and Mollie were doing as he leaned against the fence. "That reminds me . . .," Blowhard said, surprising no one, ". . . of the time a famous ancestor of mine was living out on the range in the West, far from anything."

The twins looked at each other, but neither of them said anything.

"Marauders had stolen their horses and burned their crops to the ground to scare them into leaving, but Grandpa Blowhard would have none of that. He still had two mules and he started a business raising mules. The two gave birth to

several more, and he was on his way. He didn't need horses at all. A mule can plow, and you can ride a mule. Grandpa supplied farmers for miles around with mules to help on their farms. Mollie is different, though. Her father was a horse and her mother was a donkey. That's why she's so smart.

As Blowhard walked back to his Humvee, Junior looked down at his fingers, counting out Blowhard's mistakes. He held up three fingers.

What mistakes did Junior think Blowhard made?

Answer on page 78.

Gorilla-Sitting

Benjamin Clayborn Blowhard came back to the fence where Junior Quicksolve and his twin cousins, Flora and Fauna, sat watching Detective Elliott Savant doing rope tricks as he sat on his dancing mule, Mollie.

Blowhard cleared his throat and then pushed his cowboy hat back on his head. Before he could open his mouth, Flora said, "I had a dream last night. It was more like a nightmare. Tell me what you think."

"Nightmares can be . . .," Blowhard interjected.

Flora continued. "I dreamed I was babysitting at an old farmhouse way out in the country. There wasn't another house for miles. Everything that could go wrong seemed to."

"That reminds me of the time I had to babysit a two-hundred-pound gorilla in the middle of the jungles of Borneo," Blowhard said.

Ignoring Blowhard and trying not to giggle, Fauna said, "What went wrong, Flora?'

"I mean everything!" Flora said. "There were three brothers! Triplets! They were all seven years old. There were two babies! Twins!"

"Twins?" Fauna said. "That can be trouble!" She looked at Junior with a devilish sparkle in her eyes. "And triplets! Wow!"

"For some reason, the mother ape had abandoned the baby, if you can think of a two-hundred pound gorilla as a baby!" Blowhard said.

"The three boys kept fighting. They made a mess of their

rooms, the kitchen, . . . the whole house! If I said something, they would run and hide. Then I would worry where they were. If I found one, another would run away. I could never corral all three of them at once! The twins kept crying! I would change one and then the other and then the first one again! I don't know what they ate!"

"So what did you do?" Junior asked.

"Well," Blowhard said, "the gorilla escaped into the jungle where the authorities were afraid . . ."

"No," Junior said. "I mean with the triplets and the twins. What did you do, Flora?"

Finally giving up on his story, Blowhard said, "Yes. What did you do?"

"Well," Flora said, "I did what anybody else would end up doing."

What was that?

Answer on page 74.

Christmas Tree Farm

Detective Elliott Savant had begun the day at a stakeout with his partner, the nervous Officer Alvin Boysenberry. They were watching the house of a suspected drug dealer. As they sat, Officer Boysenberry sipped coffee from a Gene Autry cowboy coffee mug that was a gift from Elliott. He held the colorful cup in both hands and sniffled quietly.

"It sounds like you have a cold," Elliott said.

"No. I think it's just the steam from the hot coffee," Boysenberry said. He sniffled again.

"No. That sounds like a bad cold coming on," Elliott said. "You probably should stay home tomorrow."

"No. I'm fine," Boysenberry said.

"No. You should stay home. You sound contagious. I don't want to get sick," Elliott insisted.

This went on all day, and Elliott finally convinced Boysenberry he was sick.

Now, Elliott was driving west on Interstate Highway 94 through beautiful, gently falling snow, and he was sitting next to Rookie Officer B. Hope Peterson, who was currently assigned to substitute for officers who called in sick. Elliott hadn't seen her for quite a while.

The thirty-mile trip beyond Chelsea and out to the Merry Christmas Tree Farm passed all too quickly.

Elliott got out of the car and pulled the earflaps of his wool cap down over his ears. He wore a red plaid coat and his shiny, black galoshes. Officer Peterson wore a short, black leather jacket and a colorfully striped stocking cap.

The Christmas tree farm, where Elliott had only several days earlier cut down his own tree, was a disaster. It was a field of nothing but small tree stumps. Local police officers were taking plaster impressions of the tracks of what was obviously a very large truck.

"They took every tree we had," Tom Trout, the owner of the farm, told them.

Elliott looked at the chain that blocked the entrance when the farm was closed. It lay on the ground to one side of the gravel drive.

"Was the chain up?" Elliott asked.

"Yes. Well . . .," Tom said. "I drove by last night on my way home from Wednesday night church, and the chain was up. It was too dark to see the trees away from the road, but I saw the tracks of the truck. I didn't think about it then, though."

"So the trees could have already been stolen?" Officer Peterson said.

"I guess so," Tom said.

"Or the truck could have been out in the back right then," Elliott said.

That would mean someone must have had a key," Officer Peterson said.

"That's right," Tom said. He turned to a young man standing nervously next to a metal apparatus with a small gasoline engine attached to it. "Sam! Was the gate locked when you got here?"

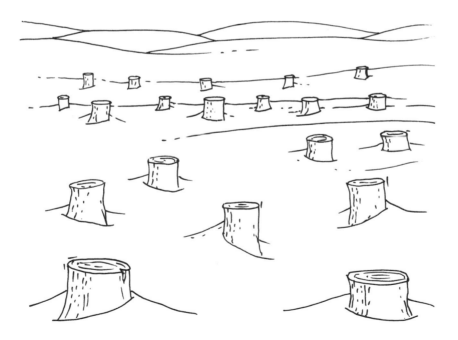

"No. It was unlocked. Fred must have left it open when he left last night," Sam said as they walked over to him.

"What's that?" Officer Peterson asked, pointing to the metal apparatus.

"That's a shaker," Sam said. "I run it."

"How does it work?" Officer Peterson asked.

Sam looked around and picked up a small scraggy tree that had been left behind. He started to pick it up. "Ouch!" he said. "I forgot my leather gloves at home."

"Here you go," Tom said. He took a pair of gloves out of his pocket and handed them to Sam.

Sam put the gloves on and set the tree on the metal apparatus and started the small engine. The tree shook frantically as the little engine roared. Needles flew off the tree in every direction. "It shakes off the old, dry and loose needles so they don't mess up your house," Sam yelled above the sound of the engine. He turned it off, and Elliott and Officer Peterson stepped aside to talk quietly to each other.

Elliott found a spot in the snow that hadn't been trampled down. He lay down on his back and spread his arms and legs out, waving them across the snow to make a snow angel.

"So there were two guys with keys," Officer Peterson said, looking down at Elliott.

"There's a reason to suspect Sam first," Elliott said. He stood up to inspect the imprint he had made in the snow.

Why suspect Sam more than Fred?

Answer on page 79.

Valentine Villainy

Elliott volunteered to work on night patrol. He was glad to learn his partner was going to be his friend Rookie Officer B. Hope Peterson.

"It was the pizza man," the manager of Mara Sofine's clothing store told them. They were surrounded by five young women who were clerks. They, along with the manager, had closed the store. "He was at just the right place at the right time. We had just collected the money."

"Can you give us some more details about exactly what happened?" Officer Peterson asked.

"Yes. Well, like I said, it was the pizza guy. He had on a ski mask. It's cold out there, so that didn't call attention to itself or upset anyone," the manager said.

"He had a pizza in his hand," one of the clerks said. "It's Valentine's Day. We thought someone was sending us a Valentine gift."

"You went to the door for the pizza?" Elliott said.

"That's right," the young woman said. "It was the second time someone was banging on the doors. We lock them at ten during the Christmas season."

"What happened the other time?" Officer Peterson asked.

"Someone knocked on the glass door at the other end of the store. Marcy went to see what they wanted. It was a guy with a bouquet of flowers. He said he had to give the flowers to Jenny. She was in the back. She always helps count the money at closing. Marcy ran back and got Jenny. The flowers were from her boyfriend. She was so excited and happy, she cried."

"Tell me about the pizza guy," Elliott said to the manager.

"He came in here right after Jenny left. He brought the pizza over to the table here, and then pulled a gun. He scooped the money into a large bag and ran out. It all happened so fast, we couldn't react," the manager said. "We were stunned. We were scared by the gun, of course."

Elliott and Officer Peterson stepped away from the others to talk. "We should talk to Jenny," Officer Peterson said.

"What are you thinking?" Elliott asked her.

"Well," she said. "When you're in love, you know a guy

from two blocks away. You know his walk, how he stands, his movements, mannerisms." She paused and looked away from Elliott for a second. "You know the sound of his voice when he whispers. You know when he's in the room before you see him."

"You do make your point," Elliott said. "So you have a suspect."

"Yes," Officer Peterson said. "I do."

Who was Officer Peterson's suspect?

Answer on page 74.

A Misty Day Murder

Dr. J. L. Quicksolve stood in the middle of the quiet street in front of a row of townhouses, which were little more from this vantage point than front doors and windows lining the whole street on either side. Detective Elliott Savant also stood in the street. They were both looking around quietly. A light rain began to fall. The two men were a strange sight in the gray morning mist. They looked a lot alike. Dr. Quicksolve was obviously the older of the two, touches of gray in his longish mustache. He wore a brown raincoat, buttoned up tightly against the weather and a hat pulled down slightly over his eyes. Elliott's black curly hair matched his bushy black mustache and showed him to be the younger of the two tall, slender men. Elliott wore shiny black galoshes and an open raincoat.

There had been a murder in townhouse number 1832. Two cars were parked along the street, Dr. Quicksolve's yellow Beetle and a small, dark sedan. The sedan belonged to the suspect.

Sergeant Shurshot gave them the details. Gerry Groanin had been stabbed to death at number 1832 at approximately ten o'clock that morning. A neighbor at number 1830 said he had watched the suspect's car from his window for some time before the murder. He said he couldn't see clearly enough to identify the person in the car, but he said the man sat in the car for several minutes after he arrived, about nine forty-five. He got out of the car and walked toward the townhouses on the even-numbered side of the road, near the 1832 address. The neighbor said he couldn't tell if the man went

in because he lost sight of him before he reached the porch. Five minutes later the man came back to his car and sat a few minutes, but he didn't leave. The police arrived just as he began to pull away.

The driver's story contradicted the neighbor's. A business acquaintance of the deceased, he claimed he had been bowling and arrived on the scene when the police came. He said he could prove it because he had called home from the bowling alley and left a message for his wife on their answering machine saying he was going to Groanin's house to talk business. He said the answering machine would be proof he only just arrived.

He was taken into custody. The scene was examined. Now only the two detectives remained.

"If he called from the bowling alley, as he claims," Elliott said, "the recorded message would be some bit of proof."

"Yes," Dr. Quicksolve said. "We need to get into the car, don't we?"

"That's right," Elliott agreed.

Why did Dr. Quicksolve want to get into the car?

Answer on page 77.

Mr. Sandman

Detective Elliott Savant sat alone in the back seat of the black and white police car. Officer Alvin Boysenberry drove the car, and Science Officer Beanie Beekerjar sat in the front passenger seat as they drove slowly through a torrential downpour.

Officer Boysenberry said, "The bank robber almost seems to be hypnotizing the tellers and disappearing with the money. Is it possible to walk up and just hypnotize someone like that?" He turned his head to look over his shoulder at Elliott.

"No, I don't think so. He doesn't have time. He walks up to the teller; he's gone in a few minutes. He might spray something that would cause a sleepiness, drowsiness, confusion," Elliott said.

"That's right," Officer Beekerjar said. "You can't just hypnotize people instantaneously."

They drove along quietly for a few minutes. The deluge had let up. The slow cadence of the wipers matched the soft music on the radio. A particularly mellow song stopped, and a breathy woman's voice said, "That's all for me tonight, but stay tuned for more romantic, easy listening and the deep, soothing voice of our very own Mr. Sandman and his "Whispering Pillows." Call Mr. Sandman to make your requests and open your heart."

Then the deep, haunting voice came on, saying, "Hello, lovers and friends. This is your Mr. Sandman, here to lead you into the misty morning's light with songs to . . ."

Elliott turned off the radio when he noticed Officer Beekerjar's eyes beginning to close. He straightened up quickly when the radio clicked off.

"Maybe the robber just talks the clerk to sleep, like Mr. Sandman on the radio," Elliott said.

This was the third bank robbery in a week, apparently by the same man. The details were simple: the thief walked in, the clerk gave him money, and the thief walked out. He wore a hat low over his eyes and changed his hair color and facial hair—a false beard or mustache—each time.

The next day was sunny and warm and began late in the morning and quite pleasantly for Elliott. He was awakened by bright sunlight streaming into his room. Then the doorbell rang, and Elliott's bulldog, Marguerite, began pulling at his bed covers.

Elliott passed through the kitchen, where he managed to pour a cup of coffee for himself and grab a dog biscuit for Marguerite without breaking stride, on his way to the door. The coffee maker had been set on a timer, and Elliott's cup was on the countertop next to Marguerite's morning treat.

Elliott opened the door to find Officer Alvin Boysenberry and Officer Beanie Beekerjar standing on his porch. He realized he was standing in the hallway in his pajamas with a coffee cup in one hand and a dog biscuit in the other. He quickly ushered them into his apartment.

"There's been another bank robbery," Officer Boysenberry said.

The bank that was robbed was in a small town. Elliott, Marguerite, Boysenberry, and Beekerjar arrived at the bank and met Officer Longarm.

"It looks like that same guy did this one," Boysenberry said. "But this time we got a description of the getaway car, and we have suspects in custody. You won't believe who they are!"

"Mr. Sandman from the radio show and Chenille Firetail were driving a car that fit the description. Miss Firetail was driving, and a county sheriff's deputy had already stopped them for speeding. Mr. Sandman said he and Miss Firetail had been at the Wompler's Lake State Park, lying on the beach for three hours, getting a little sun and waiting for the water to warm up," Officer Longarm said. "The other suspects are a couple who said they were out for a drive. He's a college professor."

"Well," Beekerjar said, "if they were really on the beach, we should find sand in their shoes, their car . . ."

"I think that beach is all grass," Elliott said. "But there is something else."

What did Elliott mean by "something else"?

Answer on page 73.

Answers

Suspicious Circumstances (Page 11)—Dr. Quicksolve couldn't be sure at that point, but it looked very suspicious. The man on the side of the road was wearing a raincoat on a sunny day, possibly hiding a specialized tool to open the car door. The raincoat and his looking away as they passed were the big clues!

Mr. Sandman (Page 69)—It occurred to Elliott that someone lying in the sun for three hours would either bear the scent of suntan lotion or be sunburned!

B & P Laundry (Page 22)—Dr. Quicksolve figured Pigeoncoff forced Bartlette to give him the number and combination to his safe deposit box before he tried to kill him. Bartlette used numbers that might have helped get him rescued. Giving each letter of the alphabet a number, these numbers would translate back to: AT LAKE, STOP P!

Valentine Villainy (Page 63)—Officer Peterson suspected the flowers could have been a diversion to draw someone out of the back office where the money was being counted. It may have been meant to draw Jenny out of the room because she might recognize the robber even with the ski mask on if he was her boyfriend!

Stolen Medals (Page 30)—Dr. Quicksolve assumed that the thief had to be someone who knew that there was no telephone in the library and also knew the medals were there, someone who knew he couldn't be seen by anyone sitting in the high-back chairs, and who knew from the one car in the driveway that only Susie was home. Dr. Quicksolve surmised that the thief stood outside the window, called from a cell phone, and made his move as soon as Susie left the room. This would have had to involve someone who had been in the house and knew something about Susie and her husband. Dr. Quicksolve wanted to see who had been in the house recently to see who the suspects were. He wanted to check if the phone had Caller I. D. to see if the thief's number was on it.

Gorilla-Sitting (Page 56)—"I woke up!" Flora said.

Beekerjar's First Case (Page 17)—Beanie Beekerjar got busy making a plaster cast of the footprints of the stranger who had approached Rachel. Then he made a cast of what looked to be the poacher's dog's prints. Then he took out his fingerprint kit and carefully got the prints from Rachel the cow! Beanie actually solved the case, and everyone decided he was born to be the science officer he had dreamed of becoming!

A Preference for Pontiacs (Page 9)—Dr. Quicksolve figured that a local mechanic or someone else who worked at a Pontiac dealership and who had access to different cars overnight was taking the license plates from similar cars and then replacing them after each robbery.

Beach Bandits (Page 47)—Elliott had decided the two wrestlers were a diversion for the thief, the man with the dogs. Elliot figured that another fight would soon begin to distract the people on the beach. At least one of the dogs— ideally, a small one in the middle of the pack—probably had been trained to search for and pick up wallets lying around with the things people left on their blankets. Elliott had not only made his wallet very interesting to the searching bandit dog, but he had marked it with the scent of mustard that would make it easy for Marguerite to find after it was stolen.

Mr. Seeotu's Briefcase (Page 27)—The culprit could have been hiding in the teacher's office when Travis cleaned the classroom. As the pencil shavings proved, Travis didn't usually go in there!

Just a Touch (Page 20)—It looked like murder, not suicide, because fingerprints should be on both sides of the paper, not just the front. You don't usually pick up a piece of paper by touching only one side. It looked like someone wiped the paper and used Jack's hand to touch the paper to make the fingerprints the police found. It also looked like Sam Stone and Honey Combs tried to look innocent by putting their names on the note, thinking the police would figure the real murderers wouldn't leave their names there!

Litter and Larceny (Page 35)—The mail had just been delivered in the late afternoon. Mail delivery is usually fairly consistent. Mr. Hogback wouldn't be looking for it in the morning if it came in the afternoon!

Dead Ringer (Page 50)—It was likely that only the employees knew about the one camera and the range of its scope, i.e., that you wouldn't be recorded if you stayed close to the wall. The fact that the owner of the store might have been able to identify his assailant could explain why he was so brutally murdered!

Rainy Day Deli (Page 13)—If they were at a secluded campsite in the rain, the car would still be quite muddy, and the mud could be traced to the camp. It they had come off the freeway, as Dr. Quicksolve suspected, the car would not be very muddy.

Bomb Threats (Page 24)—Dr. Quicksolve remembered another case where the fingerprints were actually found on the pages of a telephone book. If the caller needed several numbers from different government buildings, he probably used the telephone book, and he might well have neglected to wipe his fingerprints off the pages!

My Stolen Car Case (Page 43)—Elliott got the number of the woman's cell phone. Then he called the number and pretended the car was for sale and he wanted to buy it. He figured the thief would be happy to sell a stolen car right away for cash. He was right! Elliott arranged a meeting to buy the car and arrested the thief instead!

A Misty Day Murder (Page 66)—Dr. Quicksolve suspected the driver could have called from his car with a recording of bowling alley sounds on a tape recorder or CD so he could use the message on his answering machine as an alibi if he didn't get away from the scene in time. That tape recording of the bowling alley sounds might still be in the car!

Elliott's Talking Dog (Page 32)—Elliott and Marguerite turned to the right. The middle man had turned to his left (their right) and said, "Let's go, Starch." So Officer Lurkin was wrong when he called the middle man Starch and the third man Coils. If the middle man was not Starch and the third man was not Coils or Starch, the middle man had to be Coils and the third man had to be Slim!

A Stolen Car and a Long Walk (Page 39)—Elliott saw two things. One boy had a towel with him. He might have wiped the steering wheel clean when he got out of the car or after the deputy showed up and went into the store. The other thing Elliott noticed was that the boy still had the soda can in his hand more than half an hour after they began walking down the road. It was a hot, summer day, and after half an hour, the soda would have been very warm and not very thirst-quenching. Elliott thought the boy might have been reluctant to give up the keys to the stolen car and might have hidden them in the soda can!

Grandpa Blowhard's Mules (Page 54)—

1. Grandpa Blowhard couldn't have made a living raising mules from mules because it takes a horse and a donkey to make a mule. Mules don't usually give birth at all!

2. Mollie was a mule, so her father was a donkey and her mother was a horse. "If it were the other way around, Mollie would be a hinny, a cross between a male horse and a female donkey.

3. Blowhard implied that horses were smarter than mules and donkeys. This isn't usually the case. Mules and donkeys are sometimes considered stubborn because they're smart enough to consider the situation before they act!

Christmas Tree Farm (Page 59)—Sam's job was to handle the prickly trees all day using the shaker. It was unlikely that he'd forget his gloves, unless he was involved in the tree theft, in which case he'd know he wouldn't need them!

INDEX